MY PRIVATES ARE PRIVATE

BY: STACEY HONOWITZ
ILLUSTRATIONS BY: JORDYN BRENNER

First published by Dog Ear Publishing
4010 W. 86th Street, Ste H
Indianapolis, IN 46268
www.dogearpublishing.net

ISBN: 978-160844-281-2

Printed in the United States of America

Hi my name is Betsy Boodle
I know I am smart, I use my noodle
I'll be your friend and let you know
If someone hurts you there's a place you can go

When I say "use your noodle"
You know I mean to use your brain
Your mind is always busy working
In the sunshine and in the rain

This book will help you understand
That lots of people will lend a hand
It's always important to want to talk
You can write things down even use some chalk

You see I am just a little girl
My hair is pretty I have some curls
I have lots of freckles on my face
There are so many there's no more space

I have lots of friends who say I'm funny
I play outside when the weather's sunny
My friends all say I've really got the smarts
Cause nobody is allowed to touch my private
parts

I have lots of games that I play at home
Sometimes I love to just chat on the phone
I love to laugh, to joke and talk
Have cookies and milk, and take long walks

I go to school, I just love to learn
I stand in lunch lines and wait my turn
I run around at recess and play kickball
When school is over I shop at the mall

In school we learn a lot of things,
How grass grows and how a telephone rings
We even draw pictures in class called art
Sometimes we talk about our body parts

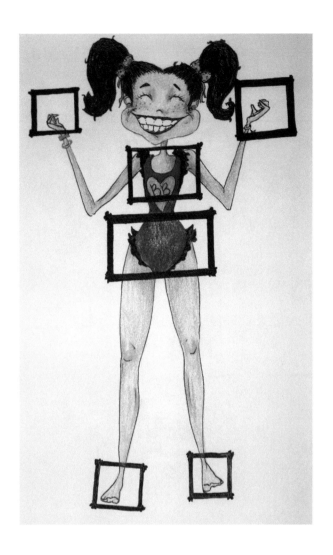

I have two feet, two legs, two arms
Just like some animals on a big farm
I also have one back, one chest
And on my front I have two breasts

I have two wrists, a waist, and ten toes
I have one head where my hair grows
Ten fingers, two ankles, and also two ears
Two eyes that sometimes shed some tears

Inside my chest I have a heart
That seems to be a special part
It's nice and red and looks real neat
The blood pumps through it to make it beat

Below my waist, above my knees
Is my PRIVATE PART that nobody sees
That is a place that nobody should touch
Even if they say I love you so much

Sometimes there are people who think its okay
They will try and put their hands down that way
But you are smart and you know that's not right
Just tell someone and they will help you fight

Tell your mom, or dad, a neighbor or friend
But whatever you choose, do not pretend
If someone touches you in a bad way
You have every right to stand up and say

DON'T TOUCH ME THERE!
You are breaking the law!
I will tell the police when I make the call
And even though I am young and short
I won't be afraid to tell the judge in court

My friends and I can get very mad,
Because we know which touches are bad
We know the meaning of the word molest
A hand, mouth or private on or in our privates
or breast

Remember my friends anyone can act nice or mean
They might want to touch you when they can't
be seen
So be aware of uncomfortable touches if you are
with them alone
And if you think there is a problem, try and get
to a phone.

Call for help, you can call the police
Your mother, your father, uncle or niece
Just make sure and tell someone,
you need to speak
It's not your fault, so don't be scared or nervous,
or meek

Make a report and don't be afraid,
Tell all the facts before your memory fades
Be a big strong kid and do the right thing
You will feel so good you'll want to sing

I did what Betsy Boodle would do
I did nothing wrong so I am reporting you
I know right from wrong and I will speak my
mind
And in the end I know I will be just fine!

LaVergne, TN USA
19 January 2010
170564LV00001B